WELCOME ABOARD!
THE CREATION OF THE *DISNEY DREAM*

WELCOME ABOARD!
THE CREATION OF THE *DISNEY DREAM*

BY JEFF KURTTI

EDITIONS

New York

For information address Disney Editions, 114 Fifth Avenue, New York, New York 10011-5690.
Editorial Director: Wendy Lefkon
Assistant Editor: Jessica Ward

This book's producers would like to thank Jennifer Eastwood, Marybeth Tregarthen, Betsy Singer, Melora Watson, Joe Lanzisero, Jeff Titelius, Tommi Lewis Tilden, and Megan Labhart.

Designed by: Jon Glick, mouse+tiger

Jeffrey Zeldman quote on page 18 from http://www.zeldman.com/2008/05/06/content-precedes-design
Charles Eames quote on page 31 from http://www.brainyquote.com/quotes/quotes/c/charleseam169187.html
Dr. Wilhelm Stekhel quote on page 40 from http://www.foodreference.com/html/qeating.html

Library of Congress Cataloging-in-Publication Data on file

ISBN 978-1-4231-2086-5
F850-6835-5-10305

First Edition
10 9 8 7 6 5 4 3 2 1
Printed in Singapore

TABLE OF CONTENTS

"I must go down to the seas again, to the lonely sea and the sky,
And all I ask is a tall ship and a star to steer her by,
And the wheel's kick and the wind's song and the white sail's shaking,
And a gray mist on the sea's face, and a gray dawn breaking."

—"Sea Fever," by John Masefield

FOREWORD

WHEN ASKED about his inspiration for *Disneyland Resort*, Walt Disney once said that he wanted to create "a family park where parents and children could have fun—together." Ever since *Disneyland* Park opened in 1955, our Company has been dedicated to creating unparalleled experiences for Guests of all ages—at five theme-park resorts around the globe that are enjoyed by millions of people each year.

In the 1990s, we embraced a new challenge: How to create a Disney family vacation experience outside our theme parks and resorts? The answer: *Disney Cruise Line* Services.

Just as Walt reinvented nearly every aspect of the amusement park, Disney and its team of Imagineers reconsidered and redefined nearly every aspect of the cruise experience. They took their inspiration from the great luxury liners of the early twentieth century, and re-imagined them as only Disney could, creating instant classics.

When our first Guests stepped aboard the *Disney Magic* Cruise Ship in 1998, they discovered an entirely new kind of Disney world—a place where families can reconnect, recharge, and create shared memories, with an array of entertainment and programming unlike anything else on the water. Where else on the high seas can you dance with pirates, dine in an animators' studio, sample the most luxurious spa treatments and see a Broadway-style musical starring your favorite *Toy Story* characters—all in the same day? It's a concept that revolutionized the industry, and it has made Disney the leader in the family cruise market.

Now, with the addition of the *Disney Dream* Cruise Ship, we are bringing the Disney Difference to more Guests in more places around the globe. This ship is longer than the Eiffel Tower and has a tonnage of 128,000, and it packs all the best that Disney has to offer.

This book is the story of the art, the craft, the skill, and the passion that have gone into the design and building of this amazing vessel. It celebrates, in words and pictures, the disciplines and talents that set *Disney Cruise Line* Services apart in its field—and the experiences and memories we create that last our Guests a lifetime.

Of course, at the heart of any great Disney Guest experience are our Cast, Crew, and Imagineers—the men and women who imagine, build, maintain, support, staff, and otherwise bring to life our properties and productions on land and at sea. They are the most important part of what makes Disney—Disney. And this new ship represents another opportunity for our people to make magic for millions of people, one guest at a time.

Welcome aboard!

Thomas O. Staggs
Chairman, Walt Disney Parks and Resorts

THE *DISNEY MAGIC*, THE *DISNEY WONDER*, AND THEIR HOME PORT

"Great ships should make the heart race. Ships are the largest things on earth that move—move not just their own bulk, but people, cargoes and, with luck, the human spirit."

—JOHN HEMINWAY,
AUTHOR OF DISNEY MAGIC:
THE LAUNCHING OF A DREAM

The graceful nautical logo of *Disney Cruise Line* Services (OPPOSITE), writ large in scale and materials on the ship's smokestack.

N MANY WAYS, it was yet another "Disney's Folly."

Much as the Disney Studio's expansion from short cartoons to features, or entry into the infant medium of television, or Walt Disney's creation of *Disneyland* Park were publicly derided as "follies," Disney's entry into the cruise business in the early 1990s was regarded with a large degree of skeptical curiosity rather than overwhelming enthusiasm.

In the intervening years, however, *Disney Cruise Line* Services has become not only a natural and comfortable component of the worldwide Disney experience, it has reached the top tier of the established cruise

industry. *Disney Cruise Line* Services was named the top large cruise ship experience by the readers of *Condé Nast Traveler* magazine in its ninth annual "Reader's Cruise Poll." In fact, *Disney Cruise Line* Services has won more than 50 different awards and accolades since launching in 1998.

Walt Disney and his wife Lillian, arriving at Montevideo, Uruguay in August 1941 (FAR LEFT), and on board the Italian Liner *Rex*, departing from San Francisco in 1935 (ABOVE).

The sketches found recurring in this volume's colorful pages, illustrate the "Disney Differences" that earn thunderous passenger praises.

The Disney standard of spotlessness is unwavering, one of pride and passion, this Difference assures that these fine craft are all shipshape and "Disney fashion."

The majesty and romance of oceangoing travel, with subtle touches of Disney iconography, and the trademark Disney excellence.

LAYING THE KEEL FOR A NEW BUSINESS

For a number of years in the 1980s, Disney had entered into licensing agreements with an existing cruise line whose three vintage ships sailed from Port Canaveral, Florida, adjacent to *Walt Disney World* Resort. Disney Characters were featured on board and in promotional materials. The public began to perceive these as "Disney's ships."

The concern within Disney, naturally, was that the high standards for the onboard experience and accommodations were not being assured and controlled in the manner that a seasoned Disney traveler would expect. The licensing agreements were terminated, and a full-scale exploration of a more substantial partnership with two established cruise lines consumed most of 1992.

Finally, a bold realization took hold: Within the functional boundaries of a cruise ship existed every discipline and expertise at which Disney had gained experience and achieved excellence—hotel; food and

The timeless feel of an ocean liner on Deck 4 (ABOVE) keeps company with the ageless icon of Mickey Mouse (RIGHT).

beverage; merchandise; entertainment; and worldwide sales. Only the ability to actually "drive the ship" was absent.

In addition, there was a strong feeling that another great Disney discipline—storytelling—was missing from modern luxury liners. They did not look like the majestic ships of our shared memory as much as behemoth floating hotels. A Disney ship would have to bring with it the nostalgia and romance of long-ago voyages—indeed, voyages that may only exist in the imagination.

The Grand Atrium of the *Disney Magic* (ABOVE), **and the *Disney Wonder*** (OPPOSITE).

DESIGNING A DREAM SHIP

More than a year of design, including competitive development among the top naval architects in the field, finally resulted in a plan for the ships that satisfied the creative and operational needs of Disney, as well as the latest developments in cruise technology.

In 1995, Disney commissioned two ships, the *Disney Magic* and the *Disney Wonder* Cruise Ships, at Fincantieri Shipyard in Italy. They were the first liners in the industry to be designed and "purpose-built" from the keel up with the goal of accommodating families.

Naturally, a sophisticated décor and style was understood as an expectation aboard a Disney ship, and an evocation of the elegant grace of early twentieth century transatlantic ocean liners was a theme that continued to surface during design development. Though not obvious, the ships also restated Disney-inspired design elements. For instance, the white superstructure, yellow trim, and two giant red funnels (each with the *Disney Cruise Line* Mickey Mouse logo) paid homage to the color palette of Mickey Mouse himself. In fact, *Disney Cruise Line* Services was granted special permission by the U.S. Coast Guard to have yellow lifeboats—in order to remain authentic to Mickey's famous shoes—instead of the regulation orange.

Not simply gaudy spectacle, elegance and luxury share space with solid comfort and intimacy on board Disney's ships. The *Disney*

Magic interior was fashioned in an art deco style, characterized by geometric designs and bold, solid colors. The interior of the *Disney Wonder* Cruise Ship was modeled in a more art nouveau style, which was distinguished by organic influences and curved shapes that avoided straight lines and right angles.

As family-oriented liners, unlike most ships of their type, the *Disney Magic* and *Disney Wonder* Cruise Ships do not include casinos. In addition, areas were meticulously designed to create discrete environments for various age groups, including toddlers, young kids, teens, and adults.

But gathering places where all ages are welcomed and celebrated are also an important element of the ships' function. Dining areas, restaurants, lounges, and theaters are a key component of life on board.

The ships each contain 877 staterooms. In standard shipboard design, public spaces are frequently given the most attention while private accommodations lean toward utility. On Disney liners, the story of majestic and nostalgic sea voyages is carried through in the interior décor, furnishings, and fittings of the staterooms.

DISNEY DETAILS

Throughout the Disney liners, subtle and sophisticated references to Disney's culture and history are everywhere. Silhouettes of Disney characters are scrolled into the yellow filigree ornamentation that stretches from bow to stern. The familiar tri-circle "Mickey" silhouette is frequently seen, including in a Mickey-shaped swimming pool. And, an abundant exhibit of varied art works are displayed, either commissioned for the ships or culled from the collections of the Walt Disney Animation Studios, Walt Disney Imagineering, and the Walt Disney Archives Photo Library. Disney novices and long-time aficionados alike can explore the Disney details on board for hours at a time.

Even the ships' horn plays the opening seven-note theme from "When You Wish Upon a Star," from Disney's 1940 animated classic *Pinocchio*.

Home Port

With all the ceremony and fanfare suitable to the occasion, the *Disney Magic* Cruise Ship began operation on July 30, 1998. A little more than a year later, the *Disney Wonder* Cruise Ship began operation August 15, 1999. Both ships call Port Canaveral, Florida, home.

Located in Brevard County, Port Canaveral is both a cargo and naval port, as well as one of the busiest passenger ports in the world. Nearly 1.3 million multi-day cruise travelers passed through the Port during 2007.

The Disney Cruise Terminal at Port Canaveral was designed to complement the Disney ships. It has an airy, streamline moderne-inspired interior, with such details as huge arched windows that offer views of the majestic liner in port; an immense terrazzo floor that is a map of the Caribbean Sea; a large-scale model of the *Disney Magic* Cruise Ship (a perfect photo spot); and an abundance of nautical details, fixtures, and décor elements.

New Ship Development Vice President for Walt Disney Imagineering Frank De

Home Port is designed to create a harmonious design statement with the *Disney Cruise Line* ships.

Heer explains that cosmetic design was not the only consideration in the Terminal: "Our Port Canaveral Terminal was designed and created by WDI 14 years ago with form *and* function in mind. Beside the external looks of a classic passenger terminal, the operational inside is designed with the Guest experience in mind. From the time they arrive to the Terminal by car or bus, the process is streamlined to make embarkation hassle-free. When disembarking, the same philosophy is used to avoid waiting lines on board the ships and within the Terminal. We have received great reviews from passengers,

crew, and government officials and our work has been an example in the industry. With the *Dream*, we continued on this successful theme and added a custom-designed parking garage and increased the luggage receiving area, complementing the design and storytelling elements of the ship. These enhancements provide Guests an even more seamless transition from land to sea during their vacation experience."

Also included is an expanded and upgraded dock to accommodate two amazing new additions to the *Disney Cruise Line* fleet.

CHAPTER TWO:
VIEW FROM THE HARBOR
A MAJESTIC SILHOUETTE

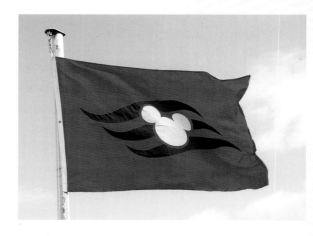

"Without an underlying story, what we do would be just decoration. We want to evoke a response in our Guests; whether that is a thought, emotion, or a memory."

—JOE LANZISERO

"YOU CAN'T TOP PIGS WITH PIGS." Walt Disney was frequently encouraged by others to simply repeat his successes. His 1933 Silly Symphony *Three Little Pigs* was such a hit that he actually produced three sequels, each with diminishing response. At this early stage in his career, Walt understood that repetition without innovation simply wasn't interesting. Over the rest of his life, Walt summarized plainly how he felt about duplication without real advancement: "You can't top pigs with pigs."

This has been a creative tenet of The Walt Disney Company for decades, and the *Disney Cruise Line* team held the same view as they approached the idea of expanding their fleet of ships and ports of call. On February 22, 2007, Disney announced that two new ships would

be added to the *Disney Cruise Line* fleet: the *Disney Dream* Cruise Ship in 2011, and the *Disney Fantasy* Cruise Ship in 2012.

Far from simply pulling the blueprints for the *Disney Magic* and the *Disney Wonder* Cruise Ships from the shelf and repeating the designs, the Disney Imagineers and their colleagues saw an enormous opportunity to expand, enlarge, update, upgrade, and improve the experience of the Disney cruise.

Kevin Cummings, Development Manager Principal of Walt Disney Imagineering, was

All plans on deck! (OPPOSITE)
Deck Plot for the *Disney Dream*.

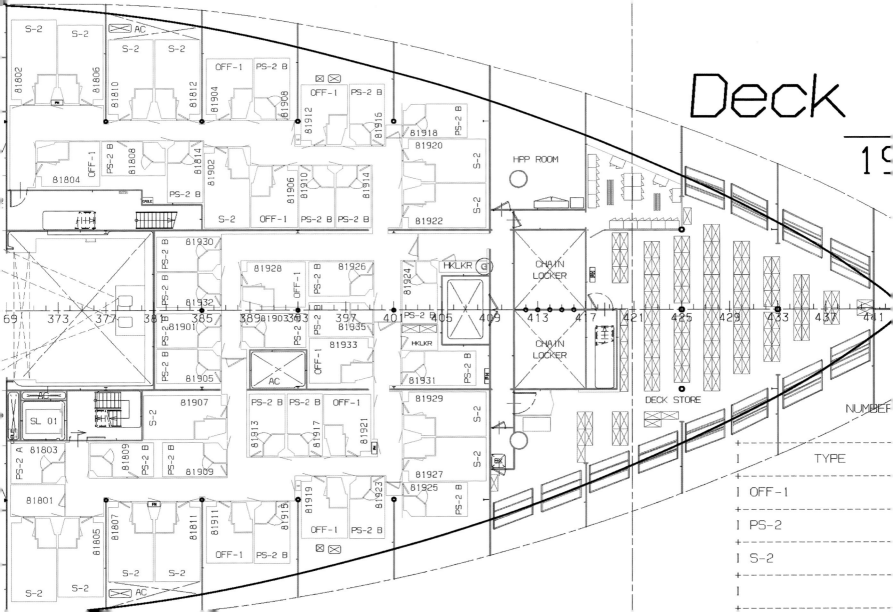

Deck

19

NUMBER

| | TYPE |
| OFF-1 |
| PS-2 |
| S-2 |

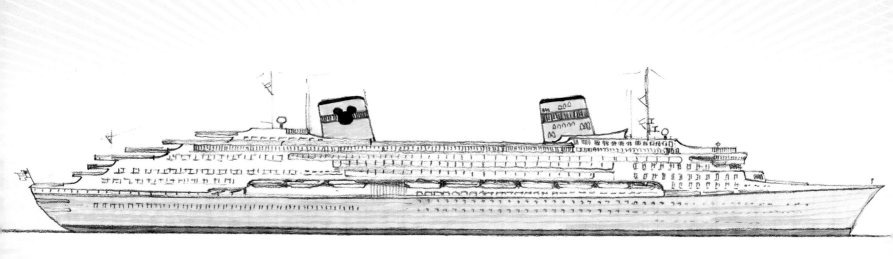

one of the experienced hands to join the new project. "Having been an Imagineer for more than twenty years, when addressing design issues I always go back and review whether I've ever come across a similar situation. We'll revisit how similar design issues have been handled—either correctly or incorrectly. Having been on the design team for our two previous ships, I've been able to take that knowledge, which often differs immensely from a typical land-based project, and use it on these two new ships."

Together the two new ocean liners more than double the capacity of the *Disney Cruise Line* fleet. These 128,000-ton ships are two decks taller than the *Disney Magic* and *Disney Wonder* Cruise Ships. They are 1,115 feet long and 121 feet wide, and have 1,250 staterooms each. Their beams measure 121 feet, with a draft of 28 feet. Overall height is 216 feet, with 14 passenger decks. Cruising speed is 22 knots (with a maximum speed of 23.5 knots). And a crew of 1,458 sees to the needs of each ship and its 4,000 passengers.

An early elevation of proposed Disney cruise ships; later designs became more refined and subtle.

Utilizing state-of-the-art design and technology, as well as a decade's worth of lessons learned from the ongoing operation of the *Disney Magic* and *Disney Wonder* Cruise Ships, the Imagineers and shipbuilders have enhanced the world-class entertainment and legendary Guest services on board. From stem to stern, the *Disney Dream* Cruise Ship offers a cruise experience that caters to the whole family.

A SIGNATURE SILHOUETTE

Like her sister ships, the *Disney Magic* and the *Disney Wonder* Cruise Ships, the *Disney Dream* Cruise Ship continues the tradition of blending the design refinement of romantically-recalled ocean liners of the past with the most current in contemporary design, resulting in one of the most stylish and spectacular cruise ships in all the oceans of the world—a unique blend of the intimate and the spectacular, the antique, and the up-to-the-minute.

Perhaps the most distinctive visual impression of the *Disney Dream* Cruise Ship is the view from afar, as passengers approach the ship in the Terminal or return from a port of call: a shape that evokes the great liners of the past while creating the lure of the fantastic promised by a Disney cruise.

"Taking a lesson from the Disney legacy of animation, we know that memorable characters can be recognized by the simplest silhouette," says Joe Lanzisero, Walt Disney Imagineering Senior Vice President, Creative. This shape represents the first communication of the great liner, and incorporates elements that symbolize

the classic ships of the past—elements that have been "designed out" of other modern luxury liners.

Details that had become passé in the modern age of shipbuilding were returned with the Disney ships. Funnels that had become unnecessary or had been hidden

Study of shapes, massing, prime viewing angles, and even art media are examined and annotated in this sketch.

to disguise their functionality are placed prominently as a component of the upper deck, angled in a manner that suggests a streamlined speed.

In recent decades, the familiar circular shape of portholes had been replaced by more typical windows, as there was no longer a practical necessity for the round-shaped apertures. But portholes and the reassuring pattern that they create across the superstructure of the ship is a part of the collective idea of a great sea voyage, so tidy rows of portholes march across the hull of the *Disney Dream* Cruise Ship.

Modern nautical engineering does not require the long, graceful prow that is an element of the *Disney Dream* design. Without this feature, however, the ship's silhouette is stunted and blocky, and

Every detail (ABOVE, BELOW, AND LEFT), **from the grandest scale to the most intimate detail, begins with a pencil, pen, or marker.**

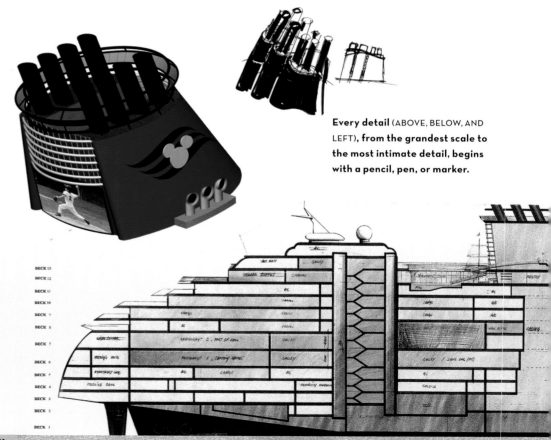

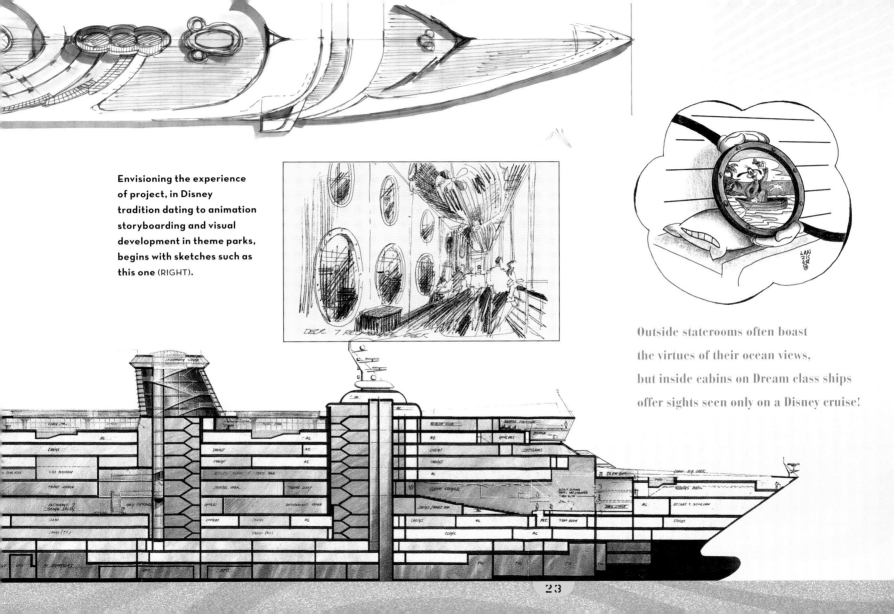

Envisioning the experience of project, in Disney tradition dating to animation storyboarding and visual development in theme parks, begins with sketches such as this one (RIGHT).

Outside staterooms often boast the virtues of their ocean views, but inside cabins on Dream class ships offer sights seen only on a Disney cruise!

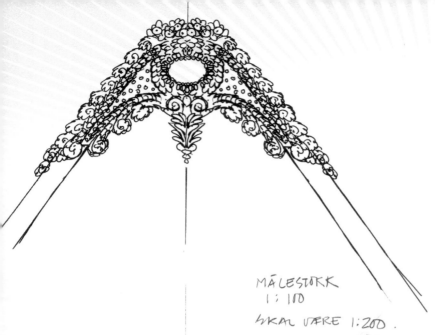

MÅLESTOKK
1: 100
SKAL VÆRE 1:200.

does not deliver the elegant impression of sophistication, speed, and forward movement. The prow that points the way to the ports of call of the *Disney Dream* Cruise Ship has no practical nautical function—but it has an imperative purpose in telling a Disney-quality story.

Great design is only as effective as the ability to bring it to functional life, and *Disney Cruise Line* Services partnered with a leader in modern shipbuilding to bring the *Disney Dream* Cruise Ship to reality.

DDC

A Partnership in Philosophy

"We carefully considered the abilities of the yard to deliver on several areas including quality, creativity, and artistic execution," shares Karl Holz, President of *Disney Cruise Line* Services & New Vacation Operations. "While economics and shipyard availability were factors, reputation was obviously important as well. Meyer Werft is known for their quality of craftsmanship in shipbuilding and we could not be more pleased with the progress and quality we've seen."

Frank De Heer sees kindred spirits in Disney's shipbuilding partner selection. "Working with a top-drawer outfit like Meyer Werft, it is easy to keep the Disney standards. Their own standards are extremely high, and work seamlessly with our own. Management of Meyer Werft simply will not accept inferior work from their own team, or from subcontractors."

Based in Papenburg, Germany, sixth-generation family-owned Meyer Werft shipyard has been a foremost shipbuilding concern for more than 200 years. Their organizational philosophy mirrors that of

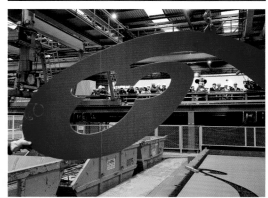

Disney: tradition combined with progress is a formula for success.

Today, Meyer Werft has an excellent international reputation for building

It is easy to forget while on board that each Disney liner is a major industrial and construction project (ABOVE AND OVERLEAF).

Captain Tom Forberg (LEFT ABOVE) and his duck-billed deckhand prepare for the laying of the *Disney Dream* keel.

sophisticated cruise liners. The shipyard is renowned in the industry for a high degree of flexibility to meet the individual needs and demands of its clients. The first steel cut, made on March 2, 2009, was for a portion of the scrollwork that decorates the exterior of the vessels.

Karl Holz says, "We are very pleased with the Meyer Werft team. We have a

Shipshape and ready to sail, the *Disney Dream* Cruise Ship (BELOW RIGHT) **takes to the waves in search of new Disney standards of seagoing excellence.**

great relationship with them, and together with Walt Disney Imagineering, we're all focused on delivering the most unique and innovative ships afloat."

On August 26, 2009, *Disney Cruise Line* Services celebrated the keel laying of the *Disney Dream* Cruise Ship. That ceremony was the first step in the *Disney Dream* Cruise Ship taking physical shape after many years of design work. In the maritime industry, the ceremony marks a momentous occasion when the first block, or section, of the ship is lowered into the building dock, and a coin is placed under the keel for good fortune.

Doing the honor of placing the coin was Captain Tom Forberg. With a distinguished maritime career aboard *Disney Cruise Line* ships, Forberg was the first crew member hired, and the captain who launched the *Disney Magic* and *Disney Wonder* Cruise Ships. Forberg is now the Master of the *Disney Dream* Cruise Ship.

After keel laying, the ship continues to take its form through a block construction process, in which pre-fabricated complete hull sections are joined in block units that are then brought together to form the ship. The *Disney Dream* Cruise Ship is comprised of 80 blocks, with the first block weighing in at approximately 380 tons.

The momentous massing and sophisticated-but-familiar styling of the superstructure of these magnificent liners provides the marquee for the entire Disney cruise experience. In this bold and colossal exterior statement, Guests, whether they are aware of it or not, are being given a preview of the combined elements of precision, craftsmanship, attention to detail, sophistication, and just plain fun that will inform every element of their voyage as they board the *Disney Dream* Cruise Ship.

"We are challenged from all directions, from all around the Company to make our designs great," Kevin Cummings says. "We have many talented people in place who review our design packages, from conceptual design through final construction documents. This variety of talents brings a wealth of knowledge that helps us move in the right direction, without having to guess and wonder which way to go. We simply call it 'The Process.' We teach this to all our consultants and builders, and they are always amazed that there is so much clarity of vision with so many people and disciplines involved."

CHAPTER THREE: BOARDING CALL

SOPHISTICATED DESIGN AND UTMOST FUNCTION

"Our Guests know that we design for them. They know that we refer to and think of them as Guests, and not as customers or clients."
—JOHN HENCH, IMAGINEER AND DISNEY LEGEND

THERE IS A FAMOUS STORY of Walt Disney standing in *Main Street, U.S.A.* Area, at *Disneyland* Park with friend and famed architect Welton Beckett. Beckett commented that there was a huge amount of architectural detail and intricate ornamentation on the second and third stories of the street, expensive features that the average Guest would never even see. In true Disney fashion, Walt is said to have replied simply, "Yeah, but they'll notice if it isn't there."

And so the tradition continues with the *Disney Dream* Cruise Ship which features a remarkable interior design that provides Guests with a warm and welcoming feel throughout.

From the majestic (but fanciful and inviting) exterior of the ship, Guests enter a wondrous and spectacular public room designed in a perfect blend of elegant early twentieth-century style and fun-filled Disney whimsy that is the design hallmark throughout the craft.

If the regal facade and evocative silhouette is the marquee for the *Disney Dream* Cruise Ship show outside, the Atrium Lobby is certainly the impressive overture upon entry.

ATRIUM LOBBY

For Guests boarding the *Disney Dream* Cruise Ship, the Atrium Lobby is meant to serve as a bellwether of their cruise experience, providing a feeling that is at once personal, visual, auditory, and emotional—a real sense of departure from one place and a stylish arrival to another.

"They say you only get one chance to make a first impression," says Joe Lanzisero. "The reaction boarding passengers have to the Atrium Lobby will be the point of

(OPPOSITE AND ABOVE) **The passenger arrival on board the *Disney Dream* Cruise Ship by way of the Grand Atrium sets the tone of elegance and attention to detail for the voyage to come.**

31

reference for the rest of their voyage, and for their expectation of everything they will see and experience after it."

Externally, the expansive three-deck space is reminiscent of splendid ocean liners from the 1920s and 1930s, with a sophisticated décor including a majestic grand staircase, oversized portholes, and soaring fluted columns with glowing capitals.

But far from being a coarse or gaudy space intended to make a grabby big statement, this area reveals remarkable craft and detail that has been brought to these Disney floating cities.

A marble floor inlaid with an intricate art deco pattern; hand-tufted rugs in blues, reds, and golds; and substantial furnishings

hundreds of sparkling crystal pendants and beads descends more than 12 feet from the Atrium ceiling.

The signature of Disney is present but never overstated. Meticulous bronze friezes lining the balconies feature subtle Disney characters, and the imposing elevator columns that ascend through the voluminous space feature elaborate metalwork crafted in an art deco pattern, with a hint of a familiar Mickey Mouse outline. Guests who possess a keen eye will also notice Disney characters ascending the bronze balustrade of the grand staircase.

However, in the tradition of her sister ships, the *Disney Dream*'s Atrium Lobby would not be complete without a more apparent and

complement the Atrium design, with a grand piano providing auditory atmosphere. Original artwork in bronze, bas-relief, and tile mosaic add further elegance. Overhead, a glittering chandelier adorned with

iconic Disney character in this welcoming space. Cast in bronze and standing nearly five feet tall atop a marble pedestal, Admiral Donald Duck pipes aboard the Guests and crew of the *Disney Dream* Cruise Ship.

A cascading inverted fountain of colorful light and glittering metallic accents (RIGHT) **provides a centerpiece for the Grand Atrium's soaring ceiling.**

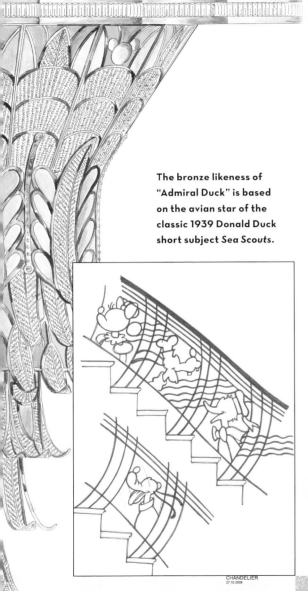

The bronze likeness of "Admiral Duck" is based on the avian star of the classic 1939 Donald Duck short subject *Sea Scouts*.

CHANDELIER
27.10.2008

Beyond the material opulence and noticeable design skill, the Atrium Lobby is also the formal greeting place where the *Disney Dream* passengers meet the most magical crew that ever sailed. Their deportment and welcome are the beginning of a personal experience that has made *Disney Cruise Line* Services an industry leader in service and satisfaction.

"Disney Cruise Line is known for outstanding Guest service on board our ships," Karl Holz says with obvious pride. "Our Crew Members are clearly our greatest asset. They are the ones who bring the magic to life for our guests each and every day."

Guest courtesy requires a special commitment by *Disney Cruise Line* Services. Holz explains, "We are committed to ensuring our Crew Members success through career development offerings whereby they have the opportunity to grow and challenge themselves professionally. Additionally, all Crew Members attend a unique orientation class called 'Traditions' that introduces them to the heritage of our company and our approach to Guest service."

WALT DISNEY THEATRE

Recalling the grandeur and luxury of the Broadway showplaces of the 1930s and 1940s, Walt Disney Theatre spans an entire three decks on the ship, providing the venue for the Broadway-style Disney live shows that have become a tradition and expectation on a Disney cruise.

"Walt Disney Theatre amazes our Guests with the rich detail and decorative touches," says Walt Disney Imagineering Creative Entertainment Vice President Michael Jung. "But we are especially excited by the state-of-the-art technology that brings the shows and experiences to life as only Disney can."

Seating more than a thousand passengers, the theater has a forty-foot-wide proscenium stage, full-flying capabilities for moveable backdrops and scenery, a projection system for animated scrims and stage lifts, and even the capacity for pyrotechnics. Additionally, the theater includes state-of-the-art digital film projection and a Dolby™ sound system.

"This theater rivals the best theatrical venues on sea or on land," Jung asserts. "We always have surprises in store for audiences,

The greatest showmen know that the entertainment begins before the performance starts, and The Walt Disney Theatre (ABOVE) immediately establishes the atmosphere for the entertainment to come.

and we've added in-theater effects that make our shows even more immersive, transformational, and magical."

The talent for the live shows equals the excellence of the facilities. "With the high expectations of our guests, we audition around the world to select only the best talent to bring our stories, characters, and magical experiences to life," says Jim Urry,

Disney Cruise Line Entertainment & Port Adventures Vice President.

Of course, the history of Disney storytelling is a unique asset in cruise entertainment. Urry explains: "Our rich Disney heritage of beloved characters, music, and stories allows us to create one-of-a-kind theatrical experiences that could only happen on a Disney ship."

BUENA VISTA THEATRE

Walt Disney Theatre is only one of two large-sized theater spaces on the *Disney Dream* Cruise Ship. Recalling the elegant yet comfortable style of the picture houses of the 1920s and 1930s, Buena Vista Theatre is a 387-seat cinema that screens first-run movies along with other popular films.

"We offer first-run Disney movies and Disney Digital 3-D. And, since we are the only cruise line in the world able to premiere movies the same day at sea as on land, our Guests are treated to a special 'PremEar at Sea' event on those occasions," Urry says.

Both Buena Vista Theatre and Walt Disney Theatre frequently hold lectures and exclusive presentations featuring special onboard Guests.

"The level of talent, passion, and diversity within our own casts are remarkable, but additionally, we are frequently joined on our cruises by world-class celebrities and performers for special event appearances, performances, and symposia," says Jung.

The exclusive, the unusual, the unexpected—and the completely

unnecessary—are some of the Disney differences that elevate the Disney cruise experience above all others, and the reason for scores of awards including the 2007 *Porthole Cruise Magazine* Readers' Choice Award for Best Family-Oriented Line.

"Being a creative and passionate community at WDI [Walt Disney Imagineering], we always like to try fresh

Presentation standards and audience comforts beyond those of the finest first-run movie houses are the standard on board the *Disney Cruise Line* ships.

and new ideas," says Bob Zalk, Show Producer and Senior Director for Walt Disney Imagineering. "It challenges us as designers and I believe our Guests really appreciate our efforts to continually push the envelope."

Innovative entertainment is obvious, or wears disguises, aboard the *Disney Cruise Line* ships; even "decorations" hold surprises.

ENCHANTED ART

Around the Atrium Lobby and throughout the *Disney Dream* Cruise Ship, Guests will discover one of those fresh and new ideas that have no practical function whatsoever—unless you feel, as the Disney Imagineers do, that surprise and fun are an absolute necessity.

Enchanted Art immerses Guests in Disney storytelling in a completely new way. A piece of art that appears to be a static animation cel from the Disney classic film *Bambi* begins to move, or a vintage photo of Walt Disney at his drawing board springs to animated life.

Throughout the public spaces of the *Disney Dream* Cruise Ship, the designers and engineers have invested an enormous amount of thought and effort into making spaces that appeal to all ages, since these are the shared spaces where every generation meets.

"This type of storytelling helps make time on the ship unique and different from the Parks," says Greg Butkus, Concept Designer Principal for Walt Disney Imagineering. "Ultimately we want to create a one-of-a-kind Disney experience."

"Stories not only come to life in the theaters and entertainment venues, but also in the many other spaces around the ship, making each member of the family feel like the cruise was created especially for them," Urry adds.

Bambi, Thumper, and Flower are among the many favorite Disney characters that come to life on board the *Disney Dream* Cruise Ship.

MAGIC   WONDER   DREAM   FANTASY

The rich artistic resources of Disney's animated fairy tales provided abundant inspiration for myriad details within the Royal Palace restaurant.

Perhaps the most frequently shared and memorable onboard space that combines the design skills of Disney with the coming together of all ages is that other "great generational equalizer"—the ancient communal activity of mealtime.

CHAPTER FOUR: SEAFARING FARE

THE SHIP'S RESTAURANTS

"Walt was also keen to make dining a good experience for Guests, not just a necessity."
—JOHN HENCH,
IMAGINEER AND DISNEY LEGEND

A one-of-a-kind interior conservatory setting greets diners visiting Enchanted Garden.

THE ORIGINS of Disney's commitment to quality food service actually date back to 1939. In designing the new Burbank headquarters of The Walt Disney Studios, a gleaming streamline moderne commissary was an important component of the plans for Walt's animation factory.

As with everything he created, there was method to Walt's food-service idea: He knew that good food at affordable prices, served adjacent to the workplace, would benefit productivity. And like everything else he affixed his name to, he demanded excellence in the food quality and service efficiency—Disney traditions that continued in Walt's plans for *Disneyland* Park, and that flourish today.

In fact, in *Walt Disney World* Resort alone, there are more than 300 places to dine (not counting the portable food carts). In all, there are more than 350 chefs on

staff at *Walt Disney World* Resort, and more than 6,000 different food items available on the property.

Food has always been an integral part of the luxury cruise experience. Some have even dubbed cruise ships "floating smorgasbords" because of the amount of food consumed on board and the constancy of its service.

On board the Disney ships, there is not only a cruise industry expectation of the type and quality of food served, there is also the expectation of the Disney standard of service effectiveness, product excellence, and nutritional value that present a challenge to the Disney culinary crew and bring a level of superiority to the Disney cruise experience.

With Disney, Guests also expect the unexpected, so *Disney Cruise Line* Services developed an innovative rotational-dining

concept that remains exclusive to the Disney fleet. While Guests "rotate" through different restaurants for dinner, their servers accompany them. Thus, Guests enjoy a variety of dining experiences with friendly, familiar, and personalized service.

The variety of onboard dining experiences on the *Disney Dream* Cruise Ship is not merely a group of nicely decorated rooms. Each of the dining areas has been designed for outstanding service and Guest comfort. Each dining room tells a unique story and offers a sophisticated integration of Disney entertainment and show quality.

"We are constantly looking at our spaces from the Guests' perspective. After all, it's for their use, their enjoyment," says Bob Zalk. "It's where their family memories are created, and then cherished. It's an important responsibility."

During the course of the meal, diners will notice their surroundings veritably blooming around them.

ENCHANTED GARDEN

Upon entering Enchanted Garden—a whimsical, restaurant inspired by the gardens of Versailles—Guests will feel as though they've arrived at a graceful cultivated conservatory.

Under a clear blue sky, a trellised garden grows, original artwork depicts lush greenery, and bouquets of custom glass "flower" light fixtures flourish from a canopy overhead. Ornamental light posts line the formal center promenade, and a central terrace features a cascading fountain, crowned by a statue of a fanciful cherub (with a mischievous resemblance to a world-famous Mouse).

After breakfast and lunch are served, a subtle change takes place in the restaurant. The sky overhead descends to a glorious and colorful sunset that soon surrenders to a twinkling field of stars. The light-fixture flowers "bloom," infused with color; wall sconces transform into exquisite folding fans; paintings are illuminated in a nocturnal glow; and the showpiece fountain takes on a shimmering starlit shine.

Eating is a cruise line sport, a hobby that has mass appeal; the Disney Difference for dining is something new at every meal!

Animator's Palate

"Animation, and the art and techniques that create it, will always be the heart of the Disney culture," says Joe Lanzisero. "I even started my own Disney career in Animation more than thirty years ago." With the launch of the *Disney Cruise Line* ships, a restaurant that brings the magic of Disney animation into the dining room for a one-of-a-kind mealtime event quickly became a signature experience of the voyage.

On the *Disney Dream* Cruise Ship, Animator's Palate has been re-imagined, developed, and enhanced to new heights of entertainment and show.

Inspired by Disney's own animation studios, the venue is filled with the behind-the-scenes materials of the animation process: character sketches, story drawings, maquettes (three-dimensional character models), paintbrushes, colored pencils, computer workstations, film strips, and other tools of the animation trade. Scenes and characters from popular Disney and Disney•Pixar films adorn the walls.

Spanning from floor to ceiling are "paintbrush" pillars and "pencil" columns. Depicted in relief on the ceiling are abstract, oversize artist's palettes and light boxes. During dinner, sparkling lights travel up the columns through fiber optic brushes to "paint" the artist's palettes with vibrant colors.

Concept development art depicting Animator's Palate with an underwater theme.

ROYAL PALACE

Like the Animator's Palate, a new dining concept making its debut on the *Disney Dream* Cruise Ship draws its inspiration from classic Disney animation. But rather than showcasing the behind-the-scenes tools and tricks of the trade from an artist's point of view, the Royal Palace brings stories told in the classics—*Cinderella*, *Snow White and the Seven Dwarfs*, *Beauty and the Beast*, and *Sleeping Beauty*—to life, immersing diners in animated luxury and storytelling opulence fit for crowned heads.

Many of the restaurant's features are modeled precisely from the animated films that inspired Royal Palace. The circular floor plan, fluted columns and iron railing work are all re-created from the romantic ballroom of Prince Charming's castle in *Cinderella*. Wall sconces are fashioned after those seen in *Beauty and the Beast*.

Additional décor in homage to the Disney animated royalty includes marble floors and luxurious carpets; a hand-blown chandelier made of glass slippers; and essential elements from each fairy tale, such as royal crests, roses, and signature tiaras. Chair backs are embellished with gilded emblems in the same motifs, and the carpet blooms in a pattern of flourishing roses.

Art nouveau portraits of princesses—Cinderella, Snow White, Belle, and Princess Aurora (Sleeping Beauty)—grace the far wall. Portholes providing spectacular views of the ocean are framed with majestic window valances, topped with sparkling tiaras.

"For me, it's about storytelling," says Zalk. "The story is the driving influence behind all that we do as Imagineers. It helps dictate all levels of design—whether it be the color palate, the lighting, the landscape, the background music—it's all connected with the story."

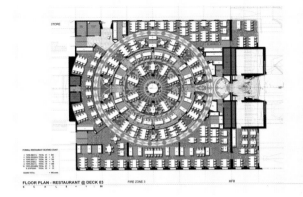

In the Royal Palace, details large and small drew their design and décor inspiration from the classic Disney animated fairy tales.

PALO

Named after the colorful poles that line the canals of Venice, Palo offers a sophisticated dining experience in a chic atmosphere—and one reserved exclusively for adult Guests. Although originating in the popular restaurant on board the *Disney Magic* and *Disney Wonder* Cruise Ships, an entirely new Palo experience has been created for the *Disney Dream* Cruise Ship.

"Our greatest challenge is always how to find the next 'thing' that will delight our Guests," Frank De Heer explains. "From the moment you put the first pencil to paper, through build and design, it is to keep that focus alive and not get complacent. That sometimes means changes midstream and thus added required resources. At the end of the day, it pays dividends when the Guests walk into a space and you see the smile on their faces. In today's fast pace of changing technology, that becomes an even greater challenge."

Palo provides a truly memorable dining experience at sea. Every seat offers a

Refinement and elegance are carefully balanced with warmth and comfort to create a unique dining experience for adults only.

beautiful ocean vista. Stylish furnishings, custom art, warm wood tones and a color palate of rich red, green, and gold jewel tones create a refined, Italian-inspired décor. And a new addition is an al fresco dining area on Palo's private teak deck.

Another supplement to the Palo experience on the *Disney Dream* Cruise Ship is a bar called Meridian. With décor inspired by the early days of sea travel, this adult-only lounge has inside seating and an exclusive outside deck.

CABANAS

"There's a mythology about California—not the state, but the state of mind, maybe even a state of relaxation," says Mike Davie, Development Manager Principal for Walt Disney Imagineering. "A fun-and-sun fantasy that everyone can relate to, whether they've ever been there or not."

Inspired by these California dreams—with uniquely Disney touches, of course—Cabanas food court is a new type of free-flow restaurant making its debut on the *Disney Dream* Cruise Ship. Featuring a variety of food and beverage

stations, Cabanas offers indoor and outdoor dining on Deck 11 aft, naturally accompanied by incredible ocean views. Across the beach-themed dining room, tables are sheltered under palm trees and beach umbrellas. Surfside décor details like kites, surfboards, and clamshell tabletops add to Cabanas' wave of California cool.

Disney details also enhance the area, including a familiar flock of possessive seagulls from the Disney•Pixar hit *Finding Nemo*, and a thirty-foot-long, hand-crafted mosaic tile wall depicts a whimsical underwater scene from that blockbuster feature.

In the evenings, Cabanas becomes a table-service casual-dining restaurant, with dinner entrees cooked to order.

Passengers of the *Disney Dream* Cruise Ship, presented with the constant service and breathtaking variety of meals, snacks, and other food service on board might be worried about a relaxing vacation turning into a huge post-cruise weight gain. But fear not: The Disney Imagineers, along with their partners at *Disney Cruise Line* Services are one step, leap, dive, splash, and putt ahead of those extra calories, with the most amazing array of onboard activities and recreation features ever to sail the seas!

CHAPTER FIVE: ON-DECK-REATION
THE DECKS, POOLS—AND AQUADUCK!

"People who cannot find time for recreation are obliged sooner or later to find time for illness."
—JOHN WANAMAKER, RETAILER AND FOUNDER OF WANAMAKER STORES

OTHER FILMMAKERS made cartoons; Walt Disney made full-length Technicolor® animated features. Other amusement parks had roller coasters, Walt Disney threaded his through a man-made alpine mountain, complete with waterfalls and a splashdown lagoon. Other attractions had wax museums and history exhibits, Walt Disney put his Guests in the middle of a fully dimensional animated pirate adventure. Other cruise lines have onboard recreation features, but true to tradition, *Disney Cruise Line* Services elevates that simple experience well beyond the ordinary.

Aboard the *Disney Dream* Cruise Ship, Deck 11 is the place to go for activities and recreation in the sun and sea. The top of *Disney Dream* Cruise Ship features three swimming pools, a toddler water-play area, and an interactive sports area. Deck 13 even features a miniature golf course.

For entire families, pool pleasures can be soaked up at Donald's Pool, while Mickey's Pool is reserved for children only. For adults, the Quiet Cove offers a little grown-up sanctuary away from adjacent, higher-volume enjoyment. All three pools are filled with fresh water rather than salt water.

A toddler water-play area, themed to the Disney•Pixar film *Finding Nemo*, features a small waterslide, water jets, and other pint-sized water features, all enclosed in a glass surround.

Goofy's Sports Deck boasts a pair of digital sports simulators and two mini-sized sports courts (called Max's Courts) where small children can play soccer and

ABOVE: **Concept development art for the toddler water-play area**

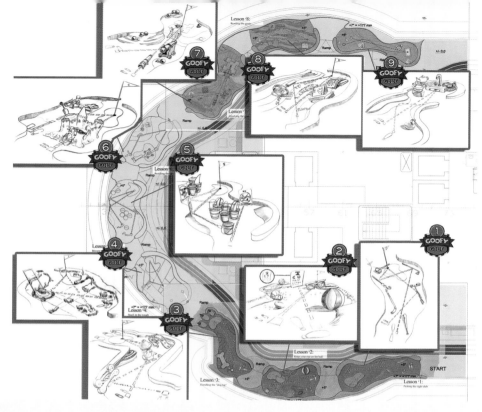

Anybody can look like a master on a golf course as goofy as this one.

basketball. There is also a full-court basketball area that can be transformed into a mini soccer pitch or volleyball court. Goofy's Golf is a nine-hole miniature golf course, inspired by Disney's intrepid sportsman and the star of the 1944 short subject, *How to Play Golf*.

The sports deck offers table tennis and foosball tables, and is encircled by a walking track.

Far from buying off-the-shelf products and simply bolting them to the ship's deck, the Imagineers must carefully integrate every element into the overall function

of the vessel. "The biggest challenge to designing innovative attractions on the new ships are the technical, environmental, and safety constraints that are necessary for this unique venue but can be difficult boxes to design within," says Imagineer Greg Butkus. "Considering every nook of space on the ship is utilized, the harsh ocean environment is not friendly to sensitive technical equipment, and the building materials are highly regulated for the security of our Guests, we end up with a very small box in which to design. But with careful navigation of all these constraints and talented designers on the team, we've been able to create even more surprises and unique magic that will thrill our Guests in every way."

The on-deck recreation areas may be a cut above the norm for cruise ship activity, but the *Disney Dream* Cruise Ship also features something of a blockbuster innovation in onboard entertainment: the cruise industry's first-ever shipboard water coaster—dubbed AquaDuck—where Guests are swept away on an exhilarating high-speed flume ride above the upper decks of the ship, and even out over the ocean.

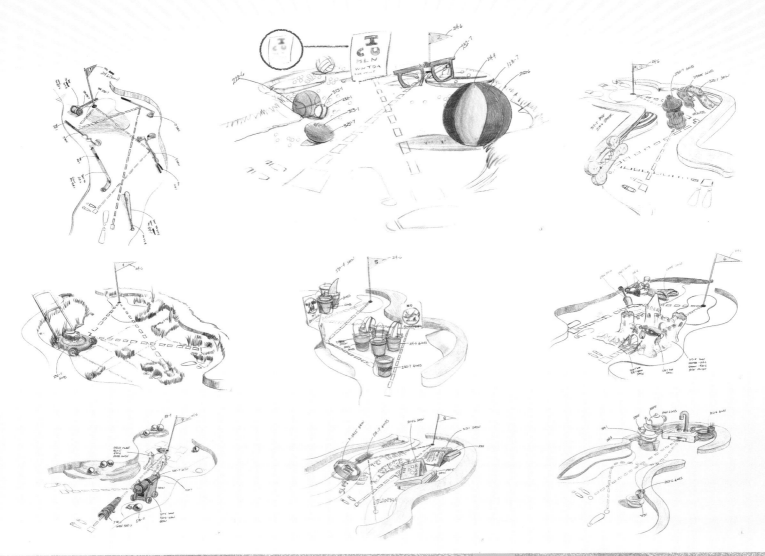

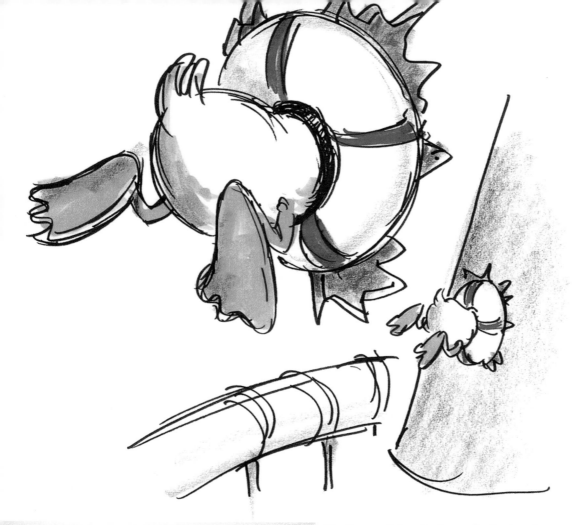

THE AQUADUCK EXPERIENCE

Stretching 765 feet in length and spanning four decks in height, AquaDuck combines the thrill of a coaster with the splashing fun of a waterslide as powerful water blasters propel Guests around the perimeter of the ship's top deck. From high atop the aft funnel, on Deck 16, Guests begin their voyage by boarding a specially designed two-person inflatable raft.

After an initial drop, Guests are suspended in a "swing out" loop that extends thirteen feet over the side of the ship. Surrounded only by the clear acrylic flume, Guests get an unobstructed view of the ocean surface 150 feet below.

Riders then experience the up-and-down sensations of a coaster, and defy gravity in a torrent of gushing water.

The flumes of AquaDuck are simultaneously functional, decorative, architectural, and kinetic, a true "landmark" of the *Disney Dream* deck.

High-powered water jets accelerate Guests upward and forward at a surging speed of about twenty feet per second, and then whisk them into an enclosed tunnel. A stretch of river rapids 335 feet in length, providing a panorama of the ocean and the ship's upper decks, washes Guests to a soaking splashdown on Deck 12.

Fantastic public spaces, exceptional and varied dining opportunities, and one-of-a-kind onboard water, sports, and recreation activities all seem like enough to fill an entire cruise adventure.

"Our Guests expect excellence in all that we produce," says Zalk. "It's a very high standard that we as Imagineers welcome as a unique and privileged challenge. Plus, it continually pushes us to keep improving our own skills along the way."

On the *Disney Dream* Cruise Ship, the foregoing fun is only the beginning of a 24/7 all-encompassing entertainment experience.

Because they entwine the horizontal space and span four decks vertically, the 765 feet of the AquaDuck seem more compact and organic to the superstructure.

Excellence in amusement
has become a Disney expectation.
These ships drench Guests in fluid fun,
soaked in inventive recreation.

Observed as a physical structure, the flume path
of AquaDuck creates an amazing sculptural
overlay to the *Disney Dream* Cruise Ship.

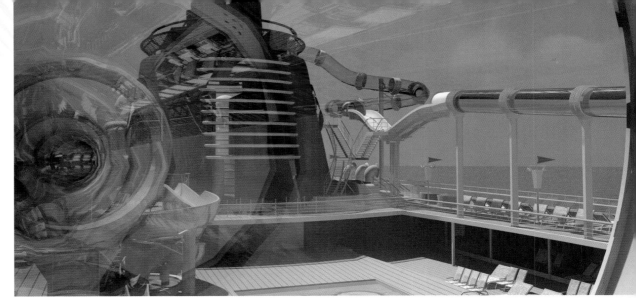

CHAPTER SIX:
ALL YOUTH ON DECK!
ACTIVITIES AND AREAS FOR YOUNGER SAILORS

"Young people are in a condition like permanent intoxication,
because youth is sweet and they are growing." —ARISTOTLE

IN THE PAST, there was a frequent tendency to regard non-adults in two categories: miniature grown-ups, or simple infants. In the entertainment business, this meant a polarization between "adult" and "kiddie" fare, with the result that often, both groups were ill-served. The continuing recognition of the nuance among youth age groups has continuously evolved over the past fifty years, first with the acknowledgment of the "teenager" in the 1950s, and the further partitioning and identification of youth sub-groups in the time since. In response, *Disney Cruise Line* Services revolutionized the cruise industry with elaborately designed youth areas, where plentiful attention has been paid to the interests and needs of specific sub-groups of youth.

Joe Lanzisero says, "The balance we confront is seeing to the specific needs of different interests and age groups, keeping their activities and 'play areas' separated, and yet keeping the entire shipboard experience seamless and appealing to everyone through the strategic use of the important public spaces and passageways. It may sound pretty straightforward, but in many ways it is like a huge, elaborate puzzle."

On board the *Disney Dream* Cruise Ship, youth spaces are naturally crucial. Not just childcare or playrooms, youth spaces are designed to inspire, entertain, and spark the imagination of children in nearly an entire deck created just for them.

It's a Small World Nursery

In the It's a Small World Nursery, infants and toddlers ages three months to three years enter a whimsical world inspired by the classic artwork by Disney Legend Mary Blair. The theme's signature fanciful style, in a quilt of shapes and bright colors, creates an inviting and comforting space for little ones.

In the Nursery's main play area, children are welcomed by three-dimensional façades resembling the Nursery's namesake Disney

The nursery is *homage* to the graphic design and color palettes of Disney Legend Mary Blair, whose work influenced Disney animation of the 1950s and theme parks of the 1960s.

attraction. There are interactive features such as horns that honk, wheels that spin, and buttons to press. A boat in the center of the room "floats" on a river pattern along the soft-surface floor, surrounded by kid-sized tables and chairs for toddlers to enjoy crafts, books, and games.

DISNEY'S OCEANEER CLUB

Disney's Oceaneer Club, open to children three-to-ten-years old, is a kid-friendly oasis that transports young Guests to the lands of Disney fairies, monsters, toys, and undersea exploration. The central rotunda, with a Never Land motif based on Disney's animated feature *Peter Pan*, is the hub of Disney's Oceaneer Club. The focal point of the rotunda is a stage where children can create and star in their very own theatrical performances, participate in storytelling sessions, and meet Disney characters such as Tinker Bell and Peter Pan.

The Disney's Oceaneer Club's rotunda also has a huge video screen for watching movies, and for live interactions with Crush, the current-surfing sea turtle from the Disney•Pixar animated motion picture *Finding Nemo*.

In Andy's Room, the world of the Disney•Pixar *Toy Story* films comes to life. Kids experience the feeling of being toy-sized as they play among larger-than-life characters, crawl through the body of Slinky® Dog, and get behind the wheel of RC Car, Andy's remote control racer.

Concept development art for Disney's Oceaneer Club illustrates a wide variety of activities for younger Guests.

Inspired by the Disney•Pixar film *Monsters, Inc.*, Monsters Academy has an elaborate climbing structure, fashioned after the film's "scare floor" where monsters Mike Wazowski and James P. "Sulley" Sullivan work. Kids can play a create-your-own monster game using magnetic pieces.

In Pixie Hollow, children visit the enchanted land inhabited by Tinker Bell and her fairy friends. The branches of a pixie tree extend overhead, with hundreds of fairy lights among the leaves, and tiny fairy houses hanging from the boughs. Here children can make crafts or dress up in fanciful fairy attire.

In Explorer Pod, inspired by the Disney•Pixar animated film *Finding Nemo*, a bright blue and yellow submarine surfaces in the middle of a room decorated with a beach theme. Inside the submarine, children can explore and play games at sixteen interactive computer stations. Outside, eight

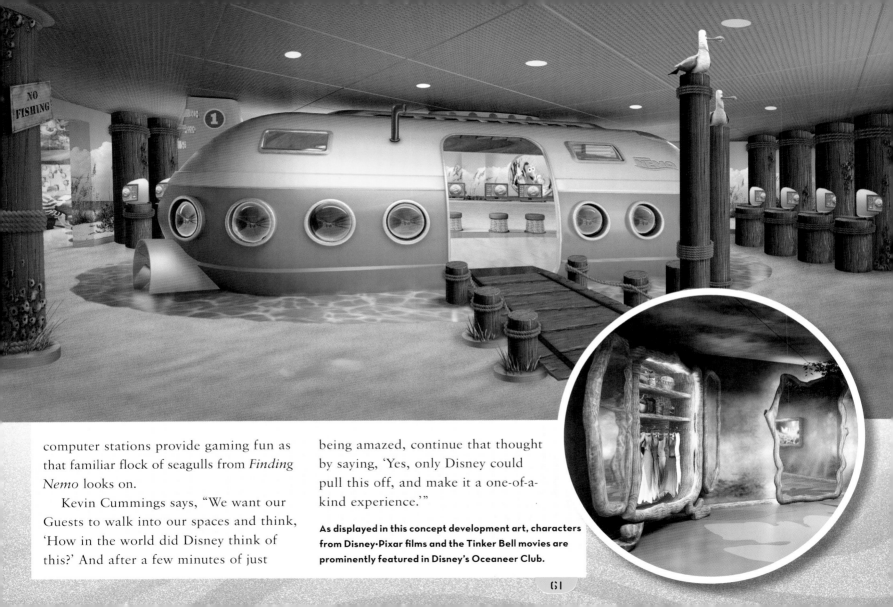

computer stations provide gaming fun as that familiar flock of seagulls from *Finding Nemo* looks on.

Kevin Cummings says, "We want our Guests to walk into our spaces and think, 'How in the world did Disney think of this?' And after a few minutes of just being amazed, continue that thought by saying, 'Yes, only Disney could pull this off, and make it a one-of-a-kind experience.'"

As displayed in this concept development art, characters from Disney·Pixar films and the Tinker Bell movies are prominently featured in Disney's Oceaneer Club.

T. LANDRY

DISNEY'S OCEANEER LAB

Disney's Oceaneer Lab is also open to three-to-ten-year-old children, offering a journey of discovery and exploration.

The main hall unfolds a story of seafaring adventure, its décor filled with nautical details, maps, maritime instruments, and salty artifacts. An illuminated compass and map glows overhead. At the main hall stage, kids can create and star in swashbuckling performances, hear stories, and watch movies.

Utilizing the same Imagineering that brings Crush to life in Disney's Oceaneer

Club, Disney's Oceaneer Lab features special scheduled visits by Disney's mischievous alien Stitch from the animated feature *Lilo and Stitch*.

The Animator's Studio features elements from both vintage and modern animator's studios, such as maquettes (three-dimensional character models), animation books, a light box table, drawing accessories, computer stations, and other tools of the animation trade. Children can use their imagination to create original, hand-drawn art, or learn how to sketch their favorite Disney character.

The Sound Studio is designed for children who appreciate and are inspired by music. Kids can create their own original tunes using special song-making software; and after composing their music and lyrics, they can record their hit.

Connecting the Disney's Oceaneer Club and the Disney's Oceaneer Lab is a workshop and science laboratory where kids can express their creativity through experiments and art projects, stretch their culinary skills, and participate in hands-on activities.

"My team brings a rich blend of participation and control into the Guest experience," Greg Butkus says, "allowing for more immersive interactions with our characters and stories. As a Guest, you don't just watch the story unfold; you are instrumental in its telling."

Telling a Disney story begins with a maxim often delivered by Marty Sklar, former International Ambassador for Walt Disney Imagineering, as the first of "Mickey's Ten Commandments": *Know Your Audience.*

Swashbuckling surroundings (OPPOSITE) **and animation activity are both a part of Disney's Oceaneer Lab.**

So, rather than lumping together all Guests under the age of eighteen, the Imagineers have also provided spaces exclusively for teens and tweens. These areas offer a getaway with the same attention to detail and Guest comfort as an adult space, where these not-quite-adults can visit with new friends, play video games, explore cutting-edge technology, or just relax in their own space.

The Edge tween club offers a space all their own to those people on the "edge" of young adulthood in a late twentieth-century "mod" setting.

TWEEN CLUB: EDGE

A tween is not quite a kid and not quite a teenager, falling directly in *between*, but with their own need for self-identification and peer socialization outside of the family group. Imagineers have created a lounge just for tweens, ages eleven to thirteen, a loft-style space with a multitude of hi-tech entertainment. Notebook computers are integrated into the design, and a massive video wall (more than eighteen feet long and nearly five feet tall) can be used for gaming, movies, or television viewing, either as one giant screen or separated into smaller individual screens.

The ship's water coaster, AquaDuck, winds through the forward funnel of the ship where three portholes in the tween club provide silhouetted views of AquaDuck's riders.

Every space on the *Disney Dream* Cruise Ship, for every age and interest, has been approached with the same thoughtfulness of design and function.

"We want our Guests to have to come back into our spaces many times just to grasp the complexity in them," Kevin Cummings says. "Like when you watch a movie over and over, and see something each time that you never saw before. That's what makes that a great movie—and in this case, a great place."

Vibe, the teens-only club, offers stylish surroundings that are both chic and comfortable, and designed for flexible use and activities.

TEEN CLUB: VIBE

A "teen-only" swipe card provides access to Vibe, a 9,000-square-foot indoor/outdoor space on Deck 5 forward. "We designed the Vibe space so teens could feel independent and comfortable away from all the adults and younger children," says Michael Davie, Walt Disney Imagineering Development Manager Principal.

The interior space is trendy, casual, and inviting. There's a fountain bar for refreshments. "We focused on incorporating all the latest technology into Vibe," adds Davie. A media room provides video gaming and movie watching on a huge video screen. And Guests can sit in built-in, oval wall "pods" designed as individual nooks for reclining and watching personal video screens or playing video games.

The technology to create and edit videos, play games, and access the onboard social media network is available at several computer stations in the lounge, or via Guests' own Wi-Fi-enabled laptops.

In the dance club area, a lighted multicolor dance floor and video wall set the stage for dancing. There is a separate stage for talent shows, karaoke contests, and dance competitions.

Outside, teens have their own private deck area that gives them an opportunity to enjoy fun in the sun, and play deck games such as ping-pong and foosball.

Family togetherness is always enhanced by a family understanding of individual tastes and needs. With so much attention and activity lavished on the younger set, doesn't it seem that the adults deserve to be spoiled and indulged in the same way?

CHAPTER SEVEN: ADULT AMUSEMENT AHOY!

NIGHTLIFE AND RESORT INDULGENCES

"If a man insisted always on being serious, and never allowed himself a bit of fun and relaxation, he would go mad or become unstable without knowing it." —HERODOTUS, ANCIENT GREEK HISTORIAN

FOR MORE THAN A DECADE, *Disney Cruise Line* Services has fought a superficial perception that Disney Cruises are for kids. Hoards of screaming, running, unsupervised hellions scurry around the decks and up and down corridors and passageways, cannonballing into the swimming pools and endlessly crying, "Marco! Polo!" at the top of their little lungs. There is no casino, and therefore, there is nothing for weary, haggard parents to do, other than eat and endure the cacophony.

Many of the adults who frequent Disney cruises—without their children or grandchildren—are perfectly happy to be "in" on the best-kept secret for grown-up passengers in the cruise business.

On the *Disney Dream* Cruise Ship while children are having the time of their lives in those elaborately themed youth areas, adults can look forward to incomparable indulgences and relaxation with exclusive areas and offerings designed just for them. With a spectacular nighttime entertainment district, exquisite dining, a deluxe spa, and a tranquil private pool, the *Disney Dream* Cruise Ship provides adults with endless ways to unwind, rejuvenate, and pamper themselves while still enjoying a wholly Disney experience.

"We pay careful attention to detail, and demand a high quality of design and materials," says Imagineering Senior Development Manager Lysa Migliorati. "We look carefully at the transition spaces

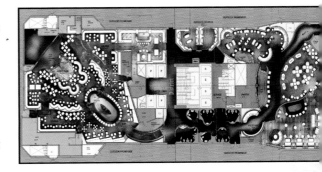

The District combines discrete spaces and varied designs into an encompassing adults-only entertainment locale.

that connect the various venues and create a cohesive relationship of the designs. We take pride in hiring the best interior design firms around the world to help us create successful spaces for all our Guests, without alienating anyone by age or category."

A show, or concert, or musician has long been the luxury cruise rage; on Disney liners, inventive venues make all the ship a stage!

The District Lounge (RIGHT) offers a perfect meeting place for passengers beginning their visit to The District. 687 Lounge (OPPOSITE) is a modern take on the traditional English Public House, a warm and casual environment that is a haven for beer lovers.

THE DISTRICT

The District is an adult-exclusive nighttime entertainment area featuring sophisticated bars and lounges, a playground for grown-ups that allows adult Guests a world all their own.

Guests visiting The District will encounter an array of experiences that stimulate all the senses, with each venue presenting its own unique design, look, feel, sounds, food, and beverages. All venues in The District are interconnected, but designed to convey a sense of discovery as Guests move from one area to another.

Travel the world without leaving the room in Skyline (ABOVE), **with its panoramic views of the world's great cities.**

SKYLINE

Skyline is an ever-changing venue that celebrates some of the world's most famous cities. Soaring "windows" along one wall give Guests a bird's-eye view of stunning city skylines such as Paris, New York, Chicago, Rio, and Hong Kong.

The chic setting is metropolitan sky bar meets luxury high-rise penthouse, complete with a digital fireplace. Lustrous woods and metal finishes are the backdrops to the seven giant screens that depict a different locale each day.

Skyline's "windows to the world" are ever-changing, as the spectacular city skylines transform from day to night, in real time, as each day progresses.

Pop the cork and enjoy a sparkling celebration in Pink, the champagne-lover's paradise inside The District.

PINK

Elegant and upscale, Pink is an intimate cocktail bar inspired by the French art nouveau style, and characterized by flowing, fluid forms. Backlit inset glass "bubbles" covering the walls create the effect of cascading, effervescent champagne. The famous pink elephants from the Disney animated classic *Dumbo* appear to dance in the bubbles.

A feature wall behind the bar, with dew drop-shaped glass in pink and gold, gives the impression of champagne bottles bursting with bubbly. Light fixtures of sculpted glass are reminiscent of champagne flutes, bar chairs seem as if they are made from sparkling crystal, and designs along the bar fascia resemble the cage around the top of a champagne bottle.

The heart of Evolution is a lighted dance floor that changes with the intensity of the music, with a colorful butterfly-shaped feature light on the ceiling above.

The bar is backlit, and features strata of layered acrylic and glass in translucent tones of orange, yellow, green, pink, and purple. Tiered banquette seating wraps around the perimeter of the room, providing a view of the entire club, the stage, and the dance floor.

This is the primary venue for large-scale evening events such as comedy acts, cabaret shows, themed dance parties, live musical performances, and other entertainment just for adults.

The transformation of a butterfly provided the design inspiration for the colors, patterns, and textures of Evolution.

EVOLUTION

The premiere venue in The District, and the main club for adult Guests is Evolution, with its interior inspired by the evolution of the butterfly.

Butterfly wing patterns on the walls and trails of light effects along the ceiling impart the feeling of butterflies in flight.

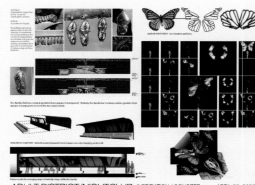

ADULT DISTRICT/NIGHTCLUB INSPIRATION / CONCEPT   APRIL 23, 2008

ICRAVE

SENSES SPA & SALON

If tranquility, pampering, and relaxation in an ocean-view environment of more than 16,000 square feet sounds like an appealing pursuit, adults can make their way to the forward section of the ship. There, spanning two decks, Senses Spa & Salon features nineteen private treatment rooms offering a menu of spa treatments and services such as massages, body wraps, and facials.

Before and after treatments, Guests can enjoy the rain forest-themed aromatherapy steam room and sauna, which offers the benefits of heat, hydrotherapy, and aroma–therapy. Or they can relax in a non-scented steam bath, steam room, or dry sauna. Two whirlpool hot tubs are available on a private teak deck.

Two lavish spa villas feature an indoor spa treatment suite connected to a private outdoor verandah with a personal whirlpool hot tub, shower, and double lounge chair.

A nearly 2,500-square-foot gym is filled with state-of-the-art exercise equipment and offers complimentary group classes such as yoga, Pilates, aerobics, stretching, and spinning.

Were it not for those ever-present hallmarks of quality, value, and uniqueness, adult Guests might forget these elegant experiences carry the Disney brand.

"At Imagineering every detail of the project is looked at by a team of experienced and talented professionals, from both a technical and creative aspect," says Lysa Migliorati. "It is the combination of the efforts from this

Comfort, serenity, and privacy replace the institutional feeling of many spas in Senses Spa & Salon.

diverse team that produces such an amazing outcome."

Whether it is an evening spent in an exciting whirl of entertainment and social activity, or the respite of a spa day at sea, both will conclude with a retreat to the comfort and tranquility of the finest passenger staterooms on the sea.

CHAPTER EIGHT: STATELY STATEROOMS
UNPARALLELED ACCOMMODATIONS

"Luxury must be comfortable, otherwise it is not luxury."

—Coco Chanel

The Verandah Stateroom (OPPOSITE) with the sea at its doors.

THE IDEA of private accommodations for Disney Guests was originated by—you guessed it—Walt Disney, in the spring of 1954. Working with Texas oilman, hotelier, and TV pioneer Jack Wrather (and his business partner Maria Helen Alvarez), Walt conceived of lodging commensurate with the sophistication of the *Disneyland* Park under construction across the street. Appealing to families without estranging adults, and establishing a level of service and mood that could justifiably be called "Disney quality" were the goals and achievements of the original Disneyland Hotel, which opened on October 5, 1955. In the years since, Disney has become a leading hotelier, operating more than 40,000 hotel rooms around the world.

Within the bulwarks of a Disney cruise liner is one of the most efficiently designed and operated luxury hotels in the world. With 1,250 rooms accommodating upward of 4,000 Guests in a fashion that can measure up to the high standards of Disney and the expectations of its Guests, the *Disney Dream* Cruise Ship not only meets, but exceeds expectations and industry standards.

Disney Cruise Line staterooms were among the first in the industry to be tailored especially for families, pioneering innovative comforts and modern features

Your stateroom is an oceangoing oasis from the moment that you get unpacked, with service so sublime and thorough that even your towel gets in on the act.

The private accommodations are no less sophisticated and well designed than the public spaces on board the *Disney Cruise Line* Ships.

not found on other cruise lines. With accommodations ranging from cozy private lodgings to grand and richly appointed suites, from rooms with added space to rooms with sweeping views, there's a stateroom to fit any need for fun and comfort. In addition, Disney staterooms are, on average, twenty-five percent larger than corresponding rooms on other cruise ships. Recognizing that families tend to travel with more luggage, *Disney Cruise Line* Services elevated bed frames to provide generous space to store suitcases and other items.

STATEROOMS

Nearly nine out of ten of the staterooms on the *Disney Dream* Cruise Ship are outside rooms, and of those, ninety percent have a private verandah. To accommodate larger families and groups traveling together, there are 1,000 adjoining staterooms. On connecting verandah staterooms, the partition between verandahs may be opened to create a larger shared balcony. The stateroom interiors are stylish and simply appointed rooms with clean lines and a crisp nautical motif, complete with beautiful wood finishes, custom fabrics and carpets, chic furnishings, original artwork, and teak accents.

Like every space on the *Disney Dream* Cruise Ship, careful design integration creates a cohesive overall design, even within very different functional areas.

"A few members from our day-to-day project team managed the comprehensive design from the very first meetings," says Kevin Cummings. "We'd sit in all the design reviews, to see what the other spaces are evolving into. We'd share opinions on different elements of the designs, or see design ideas from one space that may trigger inspirations for others.

"We would go on 'design trips,' to all the designers' studios, to see how each space was progressing, and to help everyone understand what the overall ship was becoming. By having a current knowledge of all the ships' spaces, it kept the global design intent of the ship in line. The *Disney Magic* and *Disney Wonder* Cruise Ships were also 'reference ships,' an integral part of the total design process of our two new ships."

VIRTUAL PORTHOLE

The *Disney Dream* Cruise Ship carries on the spirit of innovation with a cruise industry first for all inside staterooms: Virtual Portholes that offer a "window" to the world with a real-time view outside the ship, corresponding to the stateroom location, either port or starboard. High-definition cameras placed on the exterior of the ship feed live video to each Virtual Porthole.

As Guests are observing the impressive outside views, they may glimpse a magical surprise. Periodically, animated Disney characters may pop by the Virtual Porthole. Characters may include Peach the starfish from the Disney•Pixar film *Finding Nemo*, or even Mickey Mouse himself.

Peach the starfish from the Disney•Pixar hit *Finding Nemo* is only one of the unusual visitors that comes into view through the virtual portholes of inside staterooms.

SUITES

The *Disney Dream* Cruise Ship also has twenty-one suites, each sumptuously appointed and designed with fashionable furnishings. All suites can connect to another stateroom, creating an exceptionally spacious living area for larger groups and families.

Disney Cruise Line signature royal suites—the Walter E. Disney Suite and the Roy O. Disney Suite—are located at Deck 12 forward of the *Disney Dream* Cruise Ship. Splendid details of the signature suites include a private teakwood verandah and sweeping ocean views through the floor-to-ceiling windows lining the main living quarters.

Astonishing luxury, spacious accommodations, and spectacular ocean views bring the height of oceangoing comfort and elegance to the *Disney Cruise Line* ships.

CONCIERGE SERVICE

On the *Disney Dream* Cruise Ship, all suite and concierge stateroom Guests enjoy the benefit of the ship's Concierge Level, which provides special services and exclusive access to dedicated areas. The Concierge Lounge is located among the concierge suites on Deck 12. From the lounge, Concierge Guests have access to a private sun deck.

The accommodations on board the *Disney Dream* Cruise Ship beg the question of why you would ever want to leave your stateroom!

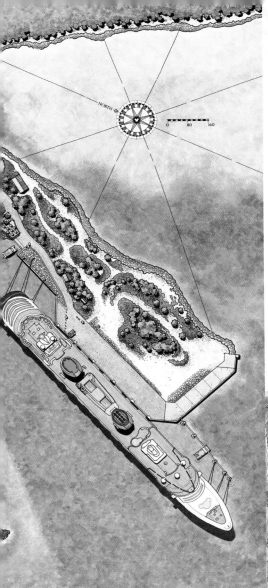

CHAPTER NINE: PORTS OF CALL

CARIBBEAN COMFORTS AT CASTAWAY CAY

"A ship in harbor is safe—but that is not what ships are built for."
—John A. Shedd, *Salt from My Attic*, 1928

With all the amenities, activities, environments, and entertainment aboard the *Disney Dream* Cruise Ship, it seems rather a surprise that anyone would actually want to get off the ship. But in addition to the top-drawer shipboard experience, the ports of call are key components of any pleasure cruise.

The *Disney Dream* Cruise Ship offers three- and four-night cruises to Nassau, the Bahamas, and *Castaway Cay* Island, Disney's private island—rated by *Disney Cruise Line* Guests as their favorite port of call.

From Plan to Paradise

Castaway Cay Island is a private island in the Bahamas that serves as an exclusive port of call for the *Disney Cruise Line* ships. Previously known as Gorda Cay, *Castaway Cay* Island is located amid the Abaco Islands in the northern Bahamas, an area first occupied in 1783 by European settlers in exile from the American Revolution.

In 1950, a pair of treasure hunters found a seventy-pound silver ingot just off the exposed shoal of the Cay. It bore the

Robinson Crusoe and the Swiss Family never had it as good as the "shipwrecked" passengers of the *Disney Cruise Line* ships at *Castaway Cay* Island.

In days gone by, a shipwreck cursed
folks to isolated misery,
but Disney only banishes cares,
cast away to luxury.

mark of Spain's King Philip IV, and beside it three coins from the same era were also found—the remains of one of scores of Spanish galleons known to have sunk in the region.

In more recent times, Gorda Cay was used as a stopover for smugglers—there is even an abandoned airstrip on the island from those days. The Cay has also been used as a movie location—the beach where Tom Hanks first encounters Daryl Hannah in *Splash* is on the island.

With the advent of *Disney Cruise Line* Services, The Walt Disney Company purchased the forsaken Cay, and the Imagineers spent two years designing and transforming it from a fairly isolated atoll into an island paradise worthy of Disney Guests.

Work included dredging the equivalent of 50,000 truckloads of sand from the depths of the Atlantic Ocean. The pier and its approaches were constructed to allow the Disney ships to dock alongside, removing the need for tenders to get the Guests ashore. To create the mooring site for the ships, workers dredged sand from a 1,700-foot channel

about thirty-five feet deep, and ranging from 250 to 400 feet wide.

The island is themed as a "castaway community," with buildings and locales designed to look as if they have been improvised from makeshift flotsam and jetsam that has found its way ashore. Some of those original castaways have lent their names and personalities to the island's facilities. Disney touches are, naturally, everywhere, including two "Nautilus" submarines (from the late, lamented *20,000 Leagues Under the Sea* attraction at *Walt Disney World* Resort *Magic Kingdom* Park) lying underwater in the snorkeling area. The haunted Flying Dutchman pirate ship, from the *Pirates of the Caribbean* films, has also been a fixture on the *Castaway Cay* horizon.

Imagineers designed *Castaway Cay* with one-of-a-kind areas and activities for every member of the family, while balancing development with the natural beauty of the island. Of the island's 1,000 acres, though, only 55 have been developed for Guest use, leaving the remaining land unspoiled and untamed.

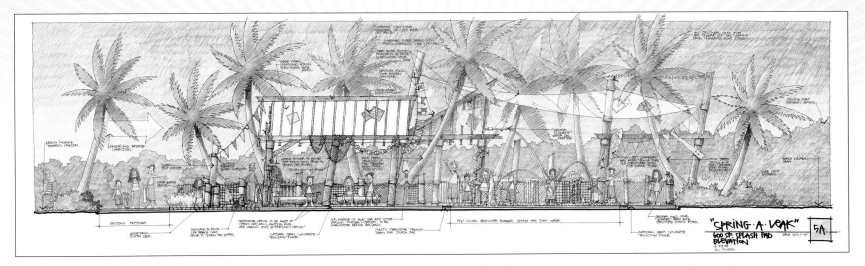

The sketch is labeled "SPRING·A·LEAK" with "600 SF SPLASH PAD ELEVATION" and "5A."

ISLAND ENHANCEMENTS

In preparation for the arrival of the *Disney Dream* Cruise Ship, *Castaway Cay* Island underwent several enhancements to provide more family fun, additional conveniences, and a sandy slice of beachside luxury—all designed to complement the existing idyllic island setting. To accommodate the new *Disney Cruise Line* ships, the dock was lengthened. An expanded family beach, a new floating water platform with slides, two land-based water play areas, new private beach cabanas, and many other upgrades have transformed *Castaway Cay* Island.

"Castaway Cay is the cruise line's gem in the ocean," Frank De Heer beams. "With fifty-percent-larger ships, we had to update the island to make that possible, from increasing the size of the berth to adding food areas and other guest amenities. This also gave us the opportunity to make existing areas even nicer and better: the play areas for the children, the shopping areas, and the beach offerings, including private cabanas. Our goal for Castaway Cay is always that Guests walk off the island at the end of a call day, which normally is their last day of a cruise, and are so satisfied that they want to return as soon as they can!"

Pelican Plunge, celebrating the island's native birds, features two waterslides on a floating platform.

IT'S A SMALL WORLD

The world is two-thirds water, and *Disney Cruise Line* Services continues to expand its destinations around the world, with existing itineraries in Alaska and along the Mexican Riviera and through the Panama Canal; in the Mediterranean region with popular ports in Spain, Italy, and France; Tunis, in Northern Africa, the island nation of Malta, and Corsica. Disney has sailed to the historic cities of Northern Europe, calling on Warnemunde, Germany, the gateway to Berlin and St. Petersburg, Russia. Enchanting Scandinavian ports like Oslo, Copenhagen, and Stockholm have also become Disney destinations.

The *Disney Dream* and the *Disney Fantasy* Cruise Ships again expand the global reach of Disney, and open the ports of the world to new generations of explorers, adventurers, and dreamers.

All in all, an admirable and noble consequence of an idea that, even a few years ago, was regarded, like *Snow White and the Seven Dwarfs* and *Disneyland* Park, as yet another "Disney Folly."

"From the beginning we set out to create the first cruise line focused on families," says Karl Holz. "Everything we did in developing Disney Cruise Line was about delivering the very best in family entertainment. We were the first to design cruise ships specifically with every member of the family in mind—kids, teens, parents, grandparents. And we built our cruise business on the company's key pillars: creativity, technology, and innovation. These, combined with Disney's master storytelling, world-class entertainment, and legendary Guest service, have resulted in a family cruise business that has become a leader within the cruise industry."

"Many years ago, when I was rather new to Imagineering, I had seen some rough concept sketches that imagined putting a small Disney-like theme park on a large ship," says Greg Butkus. "This converted supertanker held small versions of the Castle, and a little Dumbo ride, and various other familiar structures, but I always thought it was such an intriguing idea and wondered what Walt would ever have thought about a theme park on a ship.

"Well, after my first visit on the *Disney Wonder* and all the wonderful new design work being done on the new *Disney Dream*, there is no question that we've successfully done just that. There may not be a Castle on the deck, but the experience is as pure as the park, and I believe Walt would be quite pleased."

"Voyage, travel, and change of place impart vigor."
—SENECA, ROMAN PHILOSOPHER

ACKNOWLEDGEMENTS

The author would like to acknowledge the support and assistance and offer sincere thanks to Denise Brown, Greg Butkus, Kevin Cummings, Mike Davie, Christie Erwin Donnan, Tom Fitzgerald, Frank De Heer, David Duffy, Leslie Goodman, Robert Hargrove, Karl Holz, Vanessa Hunt, Gayle Jacob, Michael Jung, Michael J. Jusko, Megan Labhart, Maureen Landry, Joe Lanzisero, Jason Lasecki, Rick Lorentz, Lysa Migliorati, Diego Parras, Mary Precourt, Andrea Recendez, Julie Robinson, Thomas Schumacher, Tom Staggs, Diane Scoglio, Jim Urry, Gregory Wolfe, and Bob Zalk.